OCTONAUTS ™

and the Whale Shark

OCTONAUTS WHO'S WHO

The daring crew of the Octopod are ready to embark on an exciting new mission!

INKLING OCTOPUS
(Professor)

KWAZII CAT
(Lieutenant)

PESO PENGUIN
(Medic)

BARNACLES BEAR
(Captain)

TWEAK BUNNY
(Engineer)

SHELLINGTON SEA OTTER
(Field Researcher)

DASHI DOG
(Photographer)

TUNIP THE VEGIMAL
(Ship's Cook)

EXPLORE . RESCUE . PROTECT

OCTONAUTS™

and the Whale Shark

SIMON AND SCHUSTER

Captain Barnacles pointed up to the Octopod's videolink – Dashi was sending some amazing new pictures to the on-board computer!
Up on the screen, the crew could see her snapping photos of squid and tropical seaweed.

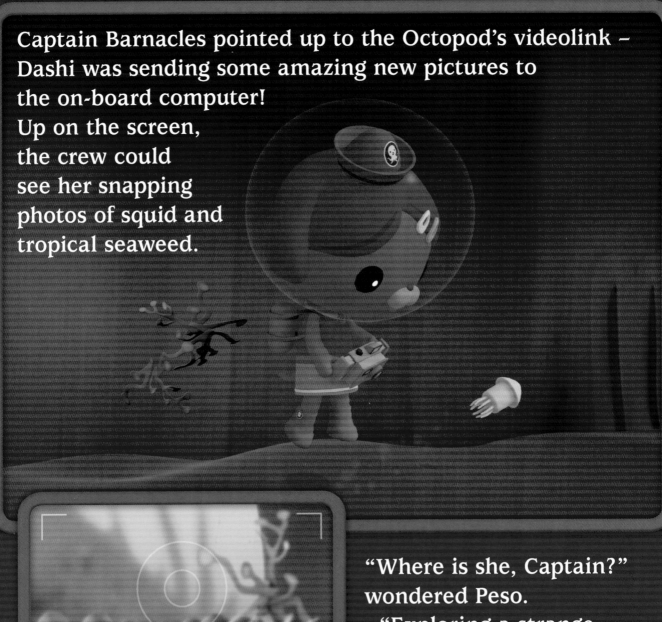

"Where is she, Captain?" wondered Peso.
"Exploring a strange underwater cave," replied Barnacles.

Shellington ran some cave data through the Octopod computer.

"The floor's red and wiggly," remarked Peso.

Shellington pushed a button and the videolink panned to a line of bumpy white rocks.

Barnacles rubbed his chin. Why did those rocks look so familiar...?

The video camera zoomed in for a closer look.
  "That's because those rocks are teeth," gulped Shellington. "And the floor is a tongue!"

Peso looked confused. "How can a cave have teeth and a tongue?"
  "Because it's not a cave..." shouted Shellington and Barnacles at the same time. **"It's a whale shark!"**

Barnacles pushed the Octopod's radio contact pad.

"Dashi!" he called. "You're not in a cave, you're in a whale shark! Get out, now!"

Dashi made a splash for the exit. The whale shark's jaws were starting to close!

"Uh-oh," she cried. "I dropped my camera."

The screen blinked, then went black.

"Peso," commanded Barnacles. "Sound the Octoalert!"

"Octonauts, to

the launch **bay**!"

"The whale shark is the
biggest fish in the sea,"
explained Shellington.
"It's so big that Dashi thought its mouth was a cave!"
  Kwazii looked cross. "How dare that dastardly beast
swallow our mate?"
  "I'm certain he didn't do it on purpose," replied Professor
Inkling. "He's a filter feeder. He just opens his mouth and
swallows whatever's there."

Tweak handed the Captain a special gadget she'd been developing for just this sort of situation.

"This is a Whale Shark Detector," she said. "It flashes if one comes near."

Barnacles, Kwazii and Peso leapt into the GUP-A. It was time to open the Octohatch!

Within seconds, the GUP-A was floating above a sandy seabed.

"That's strange," remarked the Captain. "According to the map the whale shark was right here. But I don't see him anywhere!"

Barnacles and Kwazii swam out to take a look around. All of a sudden the giant fish glided through the gloom, swallowing the pair in a single gulp!

Kwazii staggered to his feet – he'd never been inside a whale shark before!

"Let's look for Dashi by going along the tongue," decided Barnacles.

The pair slowly made their way past the whale's gills, then squeezed through a pink, spongy wall.

Alone on the GUP-A, poor Peso was starting to panic. He'd lost radio contact with his friends and now the whale shark was groaning at him!

"WWOOOOO ~ WWW!"

"You must be sick!" gasped the medic, reaching for his bag.
Peso didn't think twice. If a sea creature was poorly, he had to go and help!

Peso swam up to the whale shark's ear.

"Everything looks fine," he decided, putting away his medical torch.

The whale moaned again. And when Peso touched his tummy he moaned twice as loud as before!

"Poor whale shark," sighed Peso. "My friends must be in there!"

The whale shark didn't have measles or chicken pox. He had Octonauts!

On the other side of the sponge wall, it was eerie and dark.
Kwazii and Barnacles staggered and slid on the gooey floor.
"We seem to have landed… somewhere,"
whispered Barnacles.

Click! Click! Click!
Kwazii jumped into
the Captain's arms.
The Octonauts
were not alone!

Click!
Dashi stepped out of the shadows,
armed with her trusty camera.
She'd been snapping shots of the
whale shark's stomach.

"Octonauts, let's get up and out!" ordered Barnacles. "Totem pole."

The trio scrambled onto each others' shoulders, heaving themselves all the way back up to the whale shark's mouth.

"Yeeooow!"

Kwazii tried to karate kick a way through the mighty beast's teeth, but its jaws were shut tight.

Outside, Peso flicked through his medical book. He had to get his friends out of the whale shark's insides!

"Aha!" he read. "'If you tickle a whale shark's gills, he opens his mouth.'"

While the medic tickled from the outside, his crewmates got ready to push from the inside. "Goochy-goochy-goo!" coaxed Peso.

"On your marks, get set, GO!" bellowed Barnacles.
All of a sudden, the Octonauts tumbled out in a
big, belchy burp!

Peso grinned. He had freed his friends and cured the
whale shark's tummy ache!

When their mission was over, the Octonauts sat down to enjoy Dashi's whale shark pictures.

"I can't decide which one to send in to National Seaographic," she smiled happily.

Shellington nodded. "They're all amazing."

Inkling clapped his tentacles. "Send each and every one!"

The next photo showed Kwazii jumping into the Captain's arms.

"Ahem," coughed Barnacles. "Actually not all of them."

Kwazii agreed. "You might want to skip a few!"

The Octopod shook with chuckles. It was a big laugh at the end of a very big adventure!

Calling all Octonauts! We didn't plan on exploring the inside of a whale shark, but I'm very glad that we did! We discovered all sorts of fascinating facts about the way this big friendly giant eats, swims and breathes.

🐙 FACT FILE: **THE WHALE SHARK**

The whale shark is the largest fish in the sea. It's not a whale, just a very large shark!

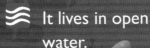 It lives in open water.

 It eats tiny floating plants and animals, and squid too.

🐙 OCTOFACTS:

1. The whale shark is enormous – as big as a school bus!

2. It swims with its mouth wide open, eating whatever floats inside.

3. The shark's gills and sponge wall keep food in and let water out.

Dive into these thrilling Octonauts books!

and the Decorator Crab

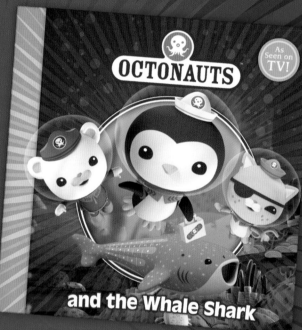

and the Whale Shark

More
great books
splash-landing
soon...

**Ready for Action
in the GUP – A!**

Meet the Crew